The Little Blue Bridge

by
Brenda Maier

pictures by
Sonia Sánchez

Scholastic Press ★ New York

Ruby's mind
was always
full of ideas.

One day, she spotted some
blueberries across the creek.

"Let's go pick berries
to bake in a pie," she said.

Everyone imagined the sweet treat.

"Okay with me," said Oscar Lee.

"Let's give it a go," said Rodrigo.

"You should stay," said José. "You're too little to cross the creek."

"I'm not too little," Ruby said.

But the boys left her behind.

When they saw Santiago, they almost turned around.

"Oh no," said Rodrigo. "Do you think he'll let us cross?"

"I'll find a way," said José, and he started across the creek.

"Why are you trip-trapping over my bridge?" bullied Santiago.

"I'm going to pick berries to bake in a pie," said José.

Santiago stood like a stone.

"I'm the boss and you can't cross . . . unless you give me a snack."

"You should wait for my brother. He packs a better snack."

"Get going then," said Santiago.

"I'll give it a go," said Rodrigo, and he started across the creek.

"Why are you trip-trapping over my bridge?" demanded Santiago.

"I'm going to pick berries to bake in a pie," said Rodrigo.

Santiago stood like a stone.

"I'm the boss and you can't cross . . . unless you give me a snack."

"You should wait for my brother. He packs a better snack."

"Get going then," said Santiago.

"Wait for me!" called Oscar Lee, and he started across the creek.

"Why are you trip-trapping over my bridge?" growled Santiago.

"I'm going to pick berries to bake in a pie," said Oscar Lee.

Santiago stood like a stone.

"I'm the boss and you can't cross . . . unless you give me a snack."

Oscar Lee thought fast.

"You should wait for my sister. She packs the best snacks!"

"Get going then," said Santiago.

Just then, Ruby started
across the creek.

"Why are you trip-trapping
over my bridge?" snarled Santiago.

"I'm going to pick
berries to bake
in a pie," said Ruby.

Santiago stood like a stone.

"I'm the boss and you can't cross . . . unless you give me a snack."

"I don't have any snacks," said Ruby.

"Then you can't cross this creek."

"I thought you might say that," said Ruby.

Ruby got right to work.

She rolled some rocks.

and laid some boards,

and gathered some vines.

Meanwhile,
Santiago stewed.
He stomped.

He spilled right into the water!

Ruby carried on.
She placed the planks
and hung the handrail.

Santiago sloshed over.
"Nice bridge," he said.
"Is it finished?"

"It's still missing
something," said Ruby.

She made a few modifications.

Santiago added one of his own.

Ruby was delighted.

"I'm hungry," she said.
"Want to get a snack?"

Together, they crossed
the creek and headed straight
for the blueberry bushes.

Much later, when the boys stumbled back, Santiago stood on a new bridge.

"Look, a better way!" said José.

"Will he let us cross though?" wondered Rodrigo.

"Let's ask him and see." said Oscar Lee.

"Actually," said Santiago. "Ruby built this bridge.

Ask HER."

Ruby stood like a stone.

"Remember when you said
I was too little to go with you?

Well, now I'm the boss,
and you can't cross . . ."

"...unless you
bake me a pie."

José's eyes grew wide.

Rodrigo's mouth watered.

Oscar Lee's stomach grumbled.

"I'll find a way," said José.

"Let's give it a go," said Rodrigo.

"Wait for me!" said Oscar Lee.

And from that day on, everyone could cross the creek.

DIFFERENT TYPES OF COMMON BRIDGES

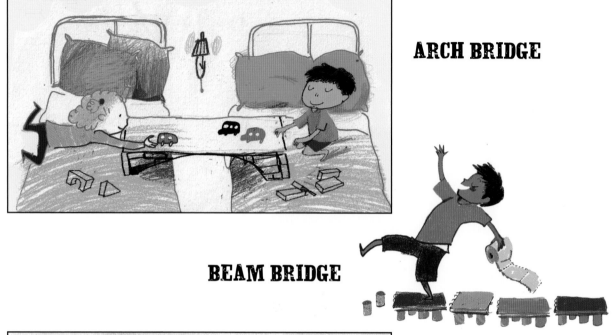

ARCH BRIDGE

BEAM BRIDGE

TRUSS BRIDGE

SUSPENSION BRIDGE

AUTHOR'S NOTE

The Little Blue Bridge is based on the Norwegian folktale you know as "The Three Billy Goats Gruff." The classic story was first recorded by Peter Christen Asbjørnsen and Jørgen Moe, two friends who wanted to collect traditional stories from their homeland. In the 1840s, Asbjørnsen and Moe published this story as part of a series called *Norwegian Folktales* (*Norske Folkeeventyr*). The title of the original Norwegian story translates roughly as "The three Billy-Goats Bruse who were going to mountain pastures to fatten themselves up." Then, in 1859, George Webbe Dasent translated the story into English and published it as part of *Popular Tales from the Norse*. During the translation, Dasent swapped out the name "Bruse" for "Gruff."

"The Three Billy Goats Gruff" has always been one of my favorite folktales. I particularly enjoy the traditional English-language versions by Paul Galdone (Clarion, 1981) and Jerry Pinkney (Little, Brown Books for Young Readers, 2017). If you'd like to read some nontraditional takes on the folktale, I suggest *The Three Billy Goats Fluff* by Rachael Mortimer and Liz Pichon (Tiger Tales, 2011), and *The Three Cabritos* by Eric A. Kimmel and Stephen Gilpin (Two Lions, 2007).

Brenda Maier

To Catren. I'd build a bridge
with you anytime. — B.M.

For Alejandro and Helena. — S.S.

Text copyright © 2021 by Brenda Maier ★ Illustrations copyright © 2021 by Sonia Sánchez ★ All rights reserved. Published
by Scholastic Press, an imprint of Scholastic Inc. *Publishers since 1920.* SCHOLASTIC, SCHOLASTIC PRESS, and associated logos are
trademarks and/or registered trademarks of Scholastic Inc. The publisher does not have any control over and does not assume
any responsibility for author or third-party websites or their content. No part of this publication may be reproduced, stored in
a retrieval system, or transmitted in any form or by any means, electronic, mechanical, photocopying, recording, or otherwise,
without written permission of the publisher. For information regarding permission, write to Scholastic Inc., Attention: Permissions
Department, 557 Broadway, New York, NY 10012. ★ This book is a work of fiction. Names, characters, places, and incidents are
either the product of the author's imagination or are used fictitiously, and any resemblance to actual persons, living or dead,
business establishments, events, or locales is entirely coincidental. ★ Library of Congress Cataloging-in-Publication Data available
ISBN 978-1-338-53801-4 ★ 10 9 8 7 6 5 4 3 2 1   21 22 23 24 25 ★ Printed in China   38 ★ First edition, April 2021

The art was created using recycled paper, charcoal pencil, pen, gouache, and a combination of traditional and digital
brushes. ★ The text type and display type were set in Sodom Regular. ★ The book was printed on 128 gsm Golden Sun matt
paper and bound at RR Donnelly Asia. ★ Production was overseen by Catherine Weening. ★ Manufacturing was supervised
by Shannon Rice. ★ The book was art directed and designed by Marijka Kostiw, and edited by Tracy Mack.